Redemption

Joanne Austen Brown

Redemption

Joanne Austen Brown

Title: Redemption

First Published 2021

This Edition: 2023 Joanne Austen Brown

Books by Joanne Austen Brown

Always Louisa ~ Book One: Always Series

Always Elspeth ~ Book Two: Always Series

Always Delia – Book Three: Always Series

Rachael's Jaunt ~ Book One: Come With Me

Molly's Laird – Book Two: Come With Me

Coming in December 2023

Glenna's Future – Book Three: Come With Me

Novellas

The Secret Letter

A Partridge in His Family Tree – Book 1 in the 12 Days of Christmas series

To my son Damien who has inspired me with his depth of character and purpose. And his magic...

The Soho Club

London 1817

"It is a strange request, your lordship." Mrs. Sarsgard stood from her chair behind her desk and wandered to the window. She looked out at the square where the light was fading. Golden light. A promise of yet another fine day for tomorrow. A clear summer with touches of rain.

"It is, ma'am, but one that I must insist on. If money is the issue..."

"No, your lordship. Money is not the issue. You are being most generous. I need to think as to who the right lady for you would be."

"I must insist on total secrecy."

"You need not concern yourself with that, sir. We honor everyone's privacy here. You can use a false name if you wish."

"Just Timothy please, Mrs. Sarsgard. I need to be me, in some respects. Just Timothy."

"Very well, your lordship. Can I suggest Friday at eight o'clock?"

"That will be suitable, ma'am."

She turned to look at him.

"Thank you, your lordship."

He stood, bowed, and left the room.

She remained deep in thought. Who would agree to his request? She had her doubts any of the women in her establishment would agree to his demand. He was a handsome man. Tall, and blond with the deepest piercing blue eyes she had ever known. But so sad. This request left her in a quandary. She returned to her desk and rang the bell. Her dear friend and business partner, Belle, came in.

"Can you organize tea please, Belle?"

"Of course, Charlotte. Mrs. Fredricks has arrived. Shall I send her in?"

"Yes please, and have tea for two sent in."

That might just work.

Hannah kept her head down as the gentleman left Mrs. Sarsgard's office. The heat rose to her face. She did not want to be recognized. Whoever he was, she had to keep her head down. At least her hat kept most of her head covered. Perhaps she had made a mistake in coming here? But what else could she do?

After a moment Miss Belle came back to her and asked her to come in to see Mrs. Sarsgard. She stood and slowly made her way into the office. Mrs. Sarsgard was standing behind her desk, immaculately dressed and looked to be in her thirties. Fine lace and silks of aquamarine. Her hair was curled in the latest fashion. But what surprised her most of all was she was so beautiful. Why with such beauty was she in the business? She mentally shook her head. Like her, she had her secrets, no doubt.

"Please Mrs. Fredricks, come and sit down. I am about to have tea. Will you join me in a cup?"

"Yes please, Mrs. Sarsgard."

"Charlotte. Please call me Charlotte."

"Thank you, Charlotte." She came over to the chair in front of the desk and sat down.

With no hesitation, Charlotte began. "Do you really think that this is the kind of job you can do?"

"I am a widow and I have nowhere else to turn."

"But I am not a poor house, madam. Here you will need to work. Work most women would not like to be doing, even with their husbands."

"If you cannot help me, then I am not sure what else I can do."

"Your husband was Benjamin Fredricks?"

"Yes, he was."

"Then I pity you, madam. The man was a beast."

"You knew him?" A sigh left her lips. "Let me guess, he was a client."

"Yes, he was, for a short time, but his behavior even disgusted us."

"I should not be surprised."

"Hannah. May I call you Hannah?"

"Yes, please do."

"Then my dear, I will be frank."

A knock at the door disturbed them.

Tea was brought in and placed on the desk in front of Charlotte. She kept her eyes down so as not to see who had come in, or the disapproving looks she knew would be leveled at her.

She kept her face turned downward.

Mrs. Sarsgard, Charlotte, stood as the person delivering the tea departed. She poured them both a cup and then sat down again.

"Your husband would beat my girls. I would not have such behavior, so we threw him out. I assume he did the same to you, but you could not get rid of him so easily. You keep your head buried, even now. Why?"

"I am embarrassed. I never thought I would find myself in this situation. Despite what he did to me, I had a home. But he left me nothing. I was not entitled to anything in his will. He did not count on a second wife."

"Do not be embarrassed. I am not embarrassed, and I understand your plight. Sometimes as women we have no choice, as you well know. Then we must do what we must to survive. You wish to survive?"

"Yes, Charlotte."

"Then, I think that we can help each other. You are not my usual type of young lady but needs must." Charlotte nodded.

"What do you mean?"

"I have a difficult situation that I need to deal with. A lord who has a particular request that is somewhat unusual. And yourself who really does not want to be here but needs help. If you want to continue to work after we have finished with the lord, then you may."

She was about to interrupt Mrs. Sarsgard but did not. The madam raised her hand to quieten her.

"You wish to survive but, my dear, you have been dealt a vicious blow. So, I am asking you to help this lord. The gentleman who just left here."

"I did not look to see who he was Charlotte, as I did not want to be recognized."

"That is good. His request is quite specific. And if you accept to do as I suggest, then you both might be saved from any further embarrassment. I will provide you with a special room which you may live in. In that room you can make yourself comfortable. Make it your home. But you will have this lord come to you. He will be your only client, for the time being."

"Dare I ask what he wants me to do, which requires me to be seeing no other clients?"

"Ah, that is the beauty of it, Hannah. He only wishes to talk."

"I beg your pardon?"

"Yes, talk. A strange request but one I understand. Will you accept?"

"Talk, you say. He will want me to listen, I assume. It seems strange, even somewhat peculiar. But yes, I think I can do that. Can I ask why?"

"Yes and no. He will speak to you as to his reasons. And I believe if you are open with him about your own situation, things may arise which will see both of you able to remove the stains on your persons, at this moment. Maintain the secrecy but tell him the truth."

"That is cryptic, Charlotte." She looked into the madam's eyes. She saw no deceit or trickery. It was the truth she told. "Yes, I will do it and thank you."

"I will arrange a contract. A simple one. You will be fed and housed, and I will pay you twenty pounds per week."

"Twenty pounds. That is so much money."

"It is but we will be paid well by his lordship."

"May I ask his name?"

"He wishes to remain anonymous so he will respond only to Timothy. Now, I will get Belle to show you to your room. Do you have any luggage?"

"I have one trunk and a bag. They are downstairs I believe."

"Then, I will have you escorted to your room. Rest and I will come and see you after dinner. Dinner will be served in your room to allow you to rest and to give you some privacy."

"Thank you, Charlotte. I am extremely grateful."

"Rest, Hannah. No thanks are needed."

Later that Evening

Hannah stood in the middle of a beautifully decorated bedroom. It was not decorated to be loud or flamboyant, which is what she had expected. The large four poster bed was off to the left. Swathed with sheer material it looked like a cloud floating in the pale blue room. A sitting room with lounges and a small table was to the right. Behind them, was a small supper table where she could eat. They were in darker shades of blue material and deep mahogany. Rich in color and expensive. She went over and sat on the three-seater. It was soft and comfortable. Leaning back, she again looked around her. She was surrounded with comfort and taste. Something that had been lacking in her life with Benjamin.

She could get used to this. But talking? And she assumed a fair bit of listening was also required of her. She shook her head. 'Timothy' came to mind. Well, there were a lot of Timothy's she knew. There were old ones, fat ones, handsome rakes, and pleasant gentlemen. But she just had to wait to see which one arrived. She gave a little shiver. Could it be the well-known rake, Timothy Mansfield St John? He knew her and she knew him. That meeting would not go well. He saw her as his enemy. She shook her head. There would be a lot of men called Timothy.

She need not be concerned. It would not be him.

"My dear Hannah, may I come in?"

"Of course, madam, I mean Charlotte."

Charlotte floated to the lounge area and sat in the great chair.

"I hope you are comfortable. It is not a room we usually use. I keep it for my friends and private guests. But for your purposes, I believe it is the best."

"The room is delightful. Far better accommodation than I am used to. My husband did not believe in fashionable accommodations."

"The more I hear of the beast the happier I am that we kicked him out."

Hannah lowered her head.

"I am sorry if my mentioning his name upsets you. That is certainly not my intention."

"Please Charlotte, there is no need to apologize. The man was a beast, and I am glad he is dead. Do I shock you? There was no love between us. I was forced to marry him when I really did not want to marry. I was also only nineteen at the time. After putting up with him for ten years, I had hoped he would give me something in his will. But his son from his first marriage inherited all and I was thrown aside."

"So, where have you been since the funeral?"

"I have stayed with a friend for a few weeks. I was able to return to the townhouse to gather my belongings. Did you know they followed me from room to room as I gathered my things? I think they hoped to catch me in the act of stealing household items."

"I am so sorry Hannah. Men will do what they can when they are threatened by a strong woman."

"I am not strong."

"On the contrary I believe you are. The ring on your finger tells me. Did they attempt to take it?"

"They did. But they would not succeed in that part. He married me, with me using my own mother's ring. My mother insisted. It was my money he wanted. Now his family has what is left of it. Some sentimental items were secreted on my being or in my luggage. I refused to allow them to search me. My cousin, Alfred, had accompanied me to be sure of the things that were legally mine, I could take. And that was precious little. Some of my mother's jewels. Most had been taken by my husband for his gambling. I had hidden some of them."

"What of your family estate?"

"It would seem my husband sold it off three years ago, and never told me. It had belonged to my father. I was the only heir. My parents died in an accident soon after I wed, and my husband took possession of it. He had lost his own estate through his gambling debts. And now have lost most of mine for the same reasons. I was angry but what could I do? Nothing. I lost a great deal in that house also. Mainly memories. But it is done." She paused. "At least I have no children, so it is only myself I need to protect now."

"What of your cousin? Would he not take you in?"

"He very much wished to, but his wife is a harpy. She refused to allow me in the house. Seems her reputation was somehow threatened with my being near her. Can you imagine what she would say if she knew what I am to become? I love my cousin. He has done what he can. I cannot blame him."

"Men. They are either beasts or cowards. Don't you agree?"

"It would seem so."

"Now, to business. His lordship is coming this Friday evening at eight. You are to dress in lingerie, but you will sit here on the main big chair. He will sit on the three-seater. There will be no candlelight. The fire will be lit. And you must wear a veil. He wants to talk. And for you to listen. He does not wish to know who you are. Not yet. You will introduce yourself as Hannah. That is all. Do you understand?"

"I do. And I am to ask him questions if I want explanations?"

"Yes, but should you have any doubts about the situation, do not hesitate to talk with me personally. Thank you, Hannah. I will have lingerie and veil brought up to you tomorrow. Rest for now."

The First Meeting

Friday *Evening*

There was a tap at the door.

"Enter." Hannah was shaking as the figure of a man entered the room. Her veil was in place, and she was glad this had been a prerequisite. She placed her hands on her lap and clung to them. He was watching her. She held her hands tighter, not wanting her shaking to be obvious to his eyes. She had even taken off her wedding ring and placed it in a safe place. She did not need it anymore. But it was her mother's, and she would keep it.

The gentleman made his way to the three-seater and sat down.

The light from the fireplace was low, but she recognized Timothy Mansfield St John immediately. She held her breath. The one man she had not wanted to appear was sitting in front of her. Now, she had to keep her identity secret so he would not rage in front of her. She did not want him to know she knew his identity. She breathed out slowly and with little sound. And so, began a new career.

"Welcome, Timothy. I understand we are here to speak together. May I invite you to start?"

"Thank you, Hannah, is it not?"

"Yes, you may call me Hannah."

"I once knew a girl called Hannah."

"It is but a name," she added.

"Thank you to agreeing to my request."

"I must admit it was a strange one but if I can help you by being a listening ear, then I will."

"Again, thank you. I will start then."

"Can I offer you a drink?" she asked.

"Thank you, but no. I want to talk. Drink will distract me."

She watched as he settled himself and began.

"This has been a burden that has been too great to bear on my own. But it is not something I want either the world or my friends and family to know. But I must speak, or I will go mad. And I thought you might listen."

He paused and she patiently waited.

"While at war, I was for a short time held prisoner."

She nodded. She watched his face as he screwed up his nose, as if uttering words that were distasteful to his mouth.

"While in the prison in France..."

She again watched as distaste and abhorrence were clearly marked.

"I will say the words, but they destroy me... I was raped, violated. A man made low."

She placed her hand to her mouth, doing what she could to prevent any noise from exiting her mouth. What? No. Shocked to the core, she was shaking again. She clutched her kerchief in her hand. The poor man was all she could think of. She closed her eyes and composed herself. He continued.

"Yes, men attacking another man. Hard to believe, I am sure, but very true. They wished for me to break, and they nearly destroyed me. I was rescued but not soon enough. For months they treated me like a sodomite. Does that shock you?"

"It shocks me that they could do that to you, yes. I am sorry."

"I do not want pity, madam. I want you to hear what I have to say and then you can hate me as I no doubt all women will now hate me."

"I do not hate you, sir, I am sorry for you, yes. But these so-called men are gone. They do not define you."

"Do they not? I cannot come near a woman without breaking into a sweat and believing they can see into my heart and know what was done to me. That is how they define me."

"I do not see you in that way. You have been damaged. But any woman worth their salt will not be affected by what has happened to you. They will love you for you."

"Even if I cannot love myself. I stink of French men. They have placed their dirt on my person and in my body. As a woman you must be able to smell them on me."

"I do not." She closed her eyes. "Timothy, I smell the sweet scent of sandalwood, and spices. The crisp scent of a freshly laundered shirt. Of clothes that are fresh and..." she said, and opened her eyes, "dirt free."

"Ah madam, you have sweet words. I wish I could believe you."

"You can, for it is the truth."

"You do not know me. So, what I say are but words to you."

She took a slow breath in. She did not yet wish to reveal herself. He might not appreciate an enemy in his midst, hearing what he did not want to share with his close friends.

"Will it help you if I sit next to you? I want to show you that I am not afraid of you or of what has happened to you."

"No, madam. Not yet. Perhaps some time in the future but not yet. Can I tell you of my past? How I grew up. Of my parents and friends. Perhaps if you know me better you can tell me what you really think."

"I am here to listen."

"Thank you. Would you mind if I take off my coat?"

"By all means."

She watched him as he stood. He undid his buttons and slipped his coat off. Again, her sense of smell was bombarded, and the aroma of sandalwood penetrated her senses. He smelled the same as he had the last time, she had seen him. When as a girl of eighteen he had asked her to dance. And to marry him. She had to say no because her parents had made other arrangements. She soon would be nineteen and married.

Again, she closed her eyes and imagined him in her arms dancing, no—waltzing, the most romantic of dances, with her. She chuckled.

"Why do you laugh, madam?"

"The sandalwood penetrates my senses."

"No doubt bringing the memories of other men to mind."

"Oh but no, sir. I can honestly say I am thinking of you alone."

"Your sugared words I do not need."

"I agree. I promise you I will only speak the truth."

"Very well, madam. But be warned if you anger me, I will retaliate."

"Timothy. Please sit down and get comfortable. Now tell me your story."

He placed his coat on the back of the lounge and then sat down.

Who was this, Hannah? This woman who spoke sweetness while he ached. He wanted the truth. He wanted her to listen and hear his pain. To look at him as if he were dirty. Not a man to be wanted.

He then noticed her hands. No jewelry. No rings, no bracelet. She sat there waiting for him. The veil may have been the wrong move. He could not see her smiles or her sneers. He would listen to her words and attempt to hear the smile. Could he? He sensed nothing for so long. Would he be able to recognize her real words?

He looked at her lingerie. Her figure beneath the lace seemed young and subtle. He closed his eyes, but his senses did not come to him. He could not picture her without seeing the French solders surrounding her, ready to attack him. The bile rose in his throat, and it stung. He felt their hands on him, and he wanted to scream. Would he always see and feel the soldiers instead of the woman in front of him? Could he not banish the image and even take a whore to his bed?

He opened his eyes to see the still seated body of the woman in the big chair, waiting.

"Timothy, believe me, you can speak the truth and I will not judge you."

Did she tell the truth?

"May I ask you, Hannah, to take my hand and tell me again that you will not judge me? And you will always tell me the truth?"

She stood and came and placed herself before him. She bent down and lifted his hand. The warmth of her fingers shot through his arm and into his soul. He knew then and there, this woman would tell him the truth, always. He sat there clinging to her hand with his head bowed. He wept. She sat down next to him and placed his head in her lap as he continued to weep.

Time disappeared. He had no sense of it. After the tears had stopped, he must have slept. He woke with her hand resting on his head. The fingertips of her other hand, the hand he had clung to, gently stroked his forehead. She had allowed him to weep as a child and stayed with him.

The feeling of deep trust in this woman took him by surprise. He had not felt this way about any woman before. Perhaps it had come close, when he had taken another Hannah into his arms and danced a waltz. She had been heaven on earth. An angel come to visit but who had been forced by her parents to marry an old man.

In his head he shook his thoughts. He could not understand why she had brought that memory to his mind. Perhaps the name. As she said it was but a name.

He sat up and took the pocket watch from his vest. He stood.

"I wish to thank you for staying with me."

"My pleasure, Timothy."

"May I see you tomorrow evening? Well, this evening as it is now after midnight."

"I am at your disposal. No. I am here for you. I will see you tomorrow."

He sensed the truth. She wanted him to come to her.

"Then dear Hannah, I will see you at eight o'clock."

He took his coat and walked to the door.

"Until this evening." And left the room.

He was gone and she wished he would walk back into the room and stay longer. She longed to take him in her arms and hug him. How could he have moved her so? Every inch of hers ached for him to be with her. She had played with his hair and studied his features as he slept. She saw the lines of pain and anger. And she wanted to kiss them. But she could not.

She went to the window and opened the curtains. She looked down and watched him enter his carriage and leave. Taking her heart with him. She slipped into her big empty bed. Oh, if only once in her life a man could take her into his arms and make love to her. That man. Timothy. She pulled her knees up to her chest and cried. All his pain and her own came crashing down on her.

A Damaged Man

S*aturday Evening 7.55 pm*

She sat in the big chair and placed her hands in her lap. He was a few minutes early, but she really did not mind.

"I want to thank you again for your tenderness last evening."

"Please do not trouble yourself, Timothy. That is why I am here."

"Perhaps, but there is a trust between us now, for which I am grateful."

"Can you please tell me more. Not so much as to what they did to you but how you coped and what you did to protect yourself while you were in prison." She really wanted to know how he kept himself alive when it would have been so easy to give up.

"It was in part due to your namesake. You may not be the Hannah that I fell in love with once upon a time, but it was she who kept me alive."

"How?" She lifted her hand to her face feeling the heat cross it. And her heart was beating like a drum.

"Although she would never be mine, I imagined she was here in London waiting for me to return. I pictured her face when I went to sleep and when I awoke. When they beat me, I imagined her healing hands on my wounds. I knew she would still love me despite what they did to me. And I stayed alive so I could return."

She stood and walked to the window. She closed the curtains. Her veil kept her secret, but she wanted to pull it off and reveal herself. But he needed to heal first. He needed to talk to remove the secrets from his heart so room could be created in his heart for her. Just for her.

She came and sat in the big chair. She studied his face again, as she had done the previous night as he slept on her lap. It was still the face she remembered. His blond hair still curled around his collar and his face. But he had pain in his eyes. Deep pain that maybe she could help remove.

"May I ask how you were freed?"

"Ah, that is a deep story."

He got up and took his coat off. She smiled that he did not seek her permission. She was glad he was comfortable enough to relax.

"Back home when the prisoners' names were made known, the French also made known they were prepared to release the wealthy sons for a price. Many fathers including mine laid out much money for our release. Why do you ask?"

"It is part of your story. You were a prisoner, yes, but not always. How did life continue till now? It is important for me to know."

"Why?"

"Please tell me, Timothy."

He sat down and eased back into the three-seater.

"My father was overjoyed to see me but shocked at my state. I had lost a great deal of weight. I had whip marks on my back and other injuries. Especially those he could not see. I could not talk. Well, I would not. How do you tell your own father what these so-called men had done to me? I just existed. What I did not know at the time was my father was ill. He was wasting away in front of me, and I did not notice."

"Your father was a great man?"

"Yes, he was."

He paused and looked at his hands. His father was deep in his thoughts. She noticed he wore his father's ring. The one that signified he was now a lord. The one his father used to wear.

"After about a month his solicitor came to see me. He was a family friend and often came to the estate to see my father. He told me my father was unwell and that I should go to his room and see him. I did but thought seeing him in his bedroom was a strange notion. But there he was in bed and looking as if he was on death's door. I ran to him and grabbed his hand and begged his forgiveness for not seeing he was ill. He reminded me that I too had not been well. He told me to take time and heal. To find a wife and settle down. The war would be forgotten."

He paused again. His thoughts deep. She stood and went to the sideboard and made his favorite drink. A whisky with just a touch of water. She brought it to him.

He took it from her and sipped it as she went and sat down again.

"How did you know?"

"I guessed."

He looked at her quizzically. He took another sip and then continued.

"I stayed with him, and we spoke about many things. I slept next to him not wanting to be far from him when the moment came. He died two days later."

"Did you tell him what they did to you?"

"How could I? He was my father. I did not want to burden him during his last hours. I promised him I would get better and run the estate to the best of my ability. And I would find a wife and marry."

"I assumed you were of the aristocracy. I also assumed you could not tell any of them what these soldiers had done to you."

"No. I could not. How could any of them fathom what we as officers had gone through."

"Were there others, other officers with similar experiences?"

He lifted his head and looked directly at her.

"Yes. You can tell when a man has experienced the deepest of pain."

"Can you? My poor Timothy."

He downed the last of his whisky and placed the glass on the table to the side of the lounge.

"What of you? May I ask you some questions?"

"You may but I have little to say that you would find interesting."

He crossed his arms and his legs.

"I find you very interesting. And I also am glad that Mrs. Sarsgard chose you to help me."

"I do not know how I am helping you, but I am happy to do so."

"My point exactly. My heart tells me that you too, have known pain. And trust me, my heart rarely speaks to me, because I can rarely hear it."

"It is true. Pain has been my friend for longer than I liked."

"Can you tell me?"

She lowered her gaze to her hands gripped tightly in her lap. The grip almost hurt. She loosened it. She would tell him but without giving herself away.

"I too was forced into a marriage I did not want. Just like your friend. He was a beast. He would rape me. He thought it so much fun to force himself on me." She watched Timothy's face grow red. "He would hit me also. Once after he had raped me, he could tell my stomach was bigger. Yes, I was pregnant. He beat me and the baby died. The bruising on my stomach lasted for months. I gave birth some hours later to a babe that was not fully formed. A girl. I called her Beth. I think I was about five months gone. I had kept it from him by making sure he raped me in a darkened room. That way too I did not need to see his face. After the babe died, I was very ill for some time and thank God, he left me alone. But soon he was back. The doctor took a great deal of care of me. He gave me solutions so I would not fall pregnant again. I wanted a child but not by this animal, my husband."

"How did you come to be here?"

"Benjamin died. But left me with nothing. Mrs. Sarsgard took me in. But enough of me. Surely there are other things we can discuss. What about your promise to your father, to marry?"

"Determined, are you, to keep yourself hidden behind the veil?"

"It was your request."

"True, I wanted to focus on your voice and manners. Not your expressions and eyes."

"Did you find a wife?"

He stood and walked to the bed. He touched the cover.

"Changing the subject again. Very well. What woman would want damaged goods? None. How could I tell them and expect them to love me in return? But I cannot take a wife and not tell them what I had experienced. I want a complete relationship. A loving one."

She stood and came to stand next to him. She placed her hand in his. At first, he pulled away, but she took hold of his hand again and held it tight.

"There will be someone."

He squeezed her hand very gently.

"I have another strange request."

"Yes?"

"Will you lie with me? Not to have sex. I just want to hold you. Hear your breath and feel your warmth."

"Certainly, Timothy."

He let go of her hand and began to undress. She slipped into the bed, leaving her veil on.

He slipped into bed, his trousers still on but with no boots or socks and his shirt hanging out. He drew up next to her and took her into his arms. Her back rested on his chest. And his groin was still. No erection.

He was damaged. A young man, she knew was in the prime of life and a woman's body tightly pressed against him brought no reaction. Again, she wanted to cry.

Soon he was asleep, his arm heavy across her body. But she loved it. She wanted him more at this moment than she had wanted any man. But he needed to heal. To become whole again.

Sometime in the night she woke and found him gone.

Bad Dreams

T*uesday Evening 7.53 pm*

He came on Saturday, Sunday, and Monday evenings. He had come and held her in his arms. No words, no touching or intimacy. Just him holding her. Now she waited for him to arrive. Would it be the same tonight?

"His lordship is here. And has asked for supper to be brought in tonight."

"Yes, he left me a note on the table."

"Is all well?"

"Yes, Charlotte. I believe so. But I would like to talk with you some time in the next few days."

"Very well, my dear. Here comes your supper and I believe his lordship is making his way upstairs."

"Thank you, Madam Sarsgard." Her reply was for the benefit of the servants who were entering the room with the food and for his lordship who was at the end of the line.

He bowed to Mrs. Sarsgard, then went to the three-seater and sat down. The servants continued to set out the supper and finally left.

"Welcome, Timothy. I hope you slept soundly last evening."

"Strangely I did. I slept longer than I have in years. And I believe it is down to you, madam. It is now three nights in a row, I have slept soundly in your arms."

She sat down again in her big chair.

"Your pale blue lace is very becoming, Hannah."

As he said her name her stomach did a somersault. She wanted to reveal herself. Tell him who she really was. But she could not. She wanted him to heal. He needed to talk more about his life since the war and why he had not yet found a wife. She had not stirred him. It could be because he was permanently damaged both in mind and soul.

"I thought supper together might help to relax us and perhaps bring more talk of things other than war."

"But the war and what it did to you, was what you wanted to talk about?"

"It is, but we can talk about us as people also, can we not?"

She got up and sat at the table opposite him. She had delayed her supper so that she could eat with him.

"I imagine we can. But I am of no import to you. I am no one."

"On the contrary, Hannah. You have allowed me to show my damaged side. The part that cannot be shared with anyone else. You have given me hope I may yet live a full life without regret."

She stared at him through her veil. She wanted to tear it off and rip it to pieces. But if she did, she could destroy all the progress they had made.

"Come, madam. Let us eat."

He poured her a glass of claret. She picked up the glass and looked at the ruby red liquid. She would have gladly shrunk and floated in the liquid than talk about herself. She lifted the glass to her mouth under the veil. It was smooth. A very good wine. As she placed the glass on the table, she decided to take matters into her own hands.

"You promised your father that you would marry. What have you done to try and fulfill that promise?"

He looked up from his food and into her veil. His features, like stone.

He did not like that question.

"I have tried. I have looked at the women who have been presented at court, but all are too young. I am thirty-three, madam. I am still young but what 'girl' would put up with such experiences I have faced?"

"It would seem you need an older woman. A widow or a spinster with some strong character traits."

"I agree. But they are few and far between, my dear. Most remarry very quickly. Or they wish to remain single. Where can I find them? And will they listen to me as you have?"

"This is not about me, Timothy. It is about finding you a wife so you can keep your promise to your father."

"Yes, that is true. But I want to be able to love them. Both in my heart and physically. Surely you would want that for me?"

"And there is the problem. I lay in your arms last night and even I could not stir you into action," she said this far more roughly than she had intended.

"Action? You want me to throw you on the bed and fill you with my seed, is that it?" His face was red, and he threw his napkin on the table.

"I apologize," she whispered. "That is not what I meant."

He was staring at her with such venom. Surely, he would not strike her?

"What do you mean then?"

"I mean that you have been violated. You are not sure you can make love to a woman again. Am I correct?"

He picked up his napkin and placed it on his lap and started to eat. She took her cue from him and began to eat. And they ate in silence for some time. She watched him as his face grew red, then became normal again. He would frown and then look at her. He was thinking deeply. But she waited to hear what he had to say. She did not want to anger him again. Anger in men frightened her. But she had to know for sure if he could physically have sex with a woman. She knew he would want to know the same.

The little minx. She had hit the nail on the proverbial head. She knew his thoughts. He so wanted her to reveal her true self.

They had slept in the same bed for three nights. Last night, he had looked at her sleeping face. The face under the veil. It was his Hannah. His Hannah. The girl who had grown into a woman. The girl he had wanted all his life. The girl he had dreamed of and who got him through that stinking war. The girl who even now excited his eyes and mind but not his groin. Not the girl but the woman. Having been treated so badly by the beast Fredricks, she had no choice but to come to a brothel.

He continued to eat. But he knew he needed to say something and soon. He picked up the bottle and poured more claret into his and her glasses.

"Yes, you are correct. I do not know if I can love any woman, even you. You sit there and tempt my mind in your sheer revealing gown. I am sure just your presence has bewitched every man who has entered this room."

"Except you are the only man who has entered this room."

"Since I hired you, yes but before?"

"You, sir, might wish to imply that I am an experienced 'madam', but I am not. I do not wish to say any more."

Ahhh, that was intriguing.

She continued to eat. Her face grew red he assumed, as every inch of her exposed body was at this moment. Under the lace she was glowing red, he knew. He had embarrassed her. But then what

Mrs. Sarsgard had said was true. She had come to her with no training but a desire to look after herself after the vicious treatment by Fredricks. And after all these years he had a chance to have her as his own. But would she take these damaged goods? Could she love a man who could not love her back? At least not physically.

They finished their supper in silence. He had to hold her again. He wanted her body against him again. To feel her and hope that her touch could stir his soul. If only she would lie in the bed with him again. Thinking about her, the war and all that had been between them had exhausted him.

"If you please Hannah, could we lay on the bed as we did the last few nights? I am tired and feel the need to rest."

He got up and undressed. He left his trousers on, took off his boots and pulled the shirt out. He slipped into the bed and pulled her against him as he had the last three nights. This felt right. This is the woman he wanted to be with. He prayed to God to allow him to be redeemed, saved by such a woman.

She was stirred from her sleep with the raised voice near her ear.

"Leave me. God save me."

He was pushing her away.

"Let go. NOOOOO." His scream echoed through her chamber.

She held onto him tight. And kept saying...

"They are not here; they cannot hurt you. You are with me, your Hannah. Think of me. They cannot hurt you anymore."

Mrs. Sarsgard came in.

"Are you alright, Hannah?"

"Yes, Charlotte. He is dreaming."

"I have seen this before. The war has hurt him badly."

"Yes, madam, it has."

The man in her arms calmed and returned to some kind of sleep. He continued to mutter but quietly and without fighting.

After a while he was deeply asleep again.

Mrs. Sarsgard left.

She did not sleep any more that night. But she held him in her arms and promised to never let go.

SCARS

Wednesday at noon

She had pretended to be asleep when Timothy rose and dressed. He opened the curtains, letting the light in, and it allowed her to see his fine figure. She knew what the next step was to be. She would discuss it with Mrs. Sarsgard to be sure she was correct and doing the right thing.

He slipped away after leaving another note on the table and she slipped into a deep sleep.

But now her late breakfast was being placed on the table. The servant had taken her verbal message to madam, asking if she could join her for a discussion.

She placed a dressing gown around her and went to the table to pour her tea. Mrs. Sarsgard entered, carrying her own cup. She came to the table and topped up her cup from the pot and sat down.

"You are troubled, my dear Hannah?"

"Yes, Charlotte. He is deeply wounded. As a prisoner...I can say no more. I do not wish to betray his confidence in me."

"You make him and me proud. This idea that you could ever be a 'madam' is a ridiculous thing."

"What do you mean?"

"You are in love with his lordship. And have been for some time."

"I will admit I knew him long ago. That I loved him then. But we are both changed."

"That may be true. But he needs you. And dare I say you need him."

"I am not sure what you mean. He can barely look at me..."

"Yet to me it is clear he is in love with you. Don't you think it may be time to reveal yourself to him?"

"No. I cannot. If I do, he will slip away from me. As far as he is concerned, I am a 'madam' in a brothel. A rich and well connected one but a brothel none the less. Let him continue to think so. Please Charlotte, I do not wish to reveal who I am yet. But I need your advice."

Charlotte crossed her arms, leaned back into the chair, and waited for her to continue. "Very well my dear, continue."

"Do I ask him to show me his scars? He was whipped and beaten. I know there are scars on his back for instance. I have felt them through his shirt. Can he move on if he bares those scars?"

"He may, my dear. But as he is not sure who you really are, he may not. I would suggest that if he asks you to take off the veil that you do so. Then you ask him to show you, his scars."

"I understand. We have reached a point of no return. We go forward or I turn away."

"Yes. But I suggest you go forward with him and see where this adventure takes you."

She nodded and picked up her cup and drained it. She poured herself another and then ate her breakfast.

She spent the afternoon creating another veil. One that hinted more at her features. She also decided to have her long blonde hair out, so it could then be seen more easily.

The lingerie she planned to wear was of the finest lace, delicate and sheer. It left no suggestion as to her sex. And as a final addition she would wear gardenia perfume. A strong and beautiful reminder of the days she knew him. He often held her close just to breathe in the mixture. She hoped now he would ask her to reveal herself.

As he came through the door, he could see she was different. Her lingerie left nothing to the imagination. Her hair was out. She still wore a veil, but he could clearly see her features through the shear material. She wanted him to know she was his Hannah. Tonight, he would let her reveal herself. Then perhaps he could reveal his love. Even if it was from a broken man.

He came and sat down in the three-seater.

“My dear Hannah, you are most beautiful tonight.”

“I thank you, my lord.”

“Can you come and kneel in front of me, my dear.”

“Yes.” She came and knelt before him. She placed her hand on his knee, and he could clearly see her smile. There was love there.

“I wish to unveil you, if I may?”

“No. Please let me reveal myself to you. A woman who loved you once.”

She lifted the veil and removed it from her head.

Again, she placed her hands on his knee.

He lifted his hands and cupped her face.

“This is no dream. You are my Hannah.”

“I am.”

She drew her face to his and he gently kissed her mouth. Sweet, tender, and rosy lips. He pulled her gently into his lap and kissed her.

My God, it was like the dreams he had while at war.

He ran his hand over her body and placed them on her plump breasts. This, her, the feel of her, the realness of her. This is all he wanted.

He picked her up in his arms and carried her to the bed. She lay there as he took his clothes off. In moments he had removed his top clothes. She sat up and pulled him to her.

"You will be mine tonight."

She laid him on the bed. Her hands wandered to the scars on his chest.

To the bullet wound that had healed on his right shoulder. She kissed the spot and his body exploded. He wanted this. He wanted her administrations. He took her hand and kissed it. She dropped to the sword wound on his left side. Her lips were over the rough scar, and she laid kisses upon it.

"Oh, my Hannah. This is what I want. This is what I need to feel. No one has ever touched my wound but doctors. You are what I want and need."

"I am here to take the fear away, my lord."

"Timothy. Please call me your Timothy as you once did."

She reached his mouth and said the word he longed to hear.

"Timothy."

She placed her tongue on his teeth, and he opened to her. The kiss was long and lustful. Both devoured each other as if they would die if they did not taste every inch of flesh.

He placed his hand under her lingerie and found the moist spot that lay between her legs. She cried out into his mouth as his fingers danced in the moisture.

"I need you," she whispered.

He placed his hand down his trousers and undid the buttons. His erect member dropped to his hand. She took it and guided his manhood to her moisture. Suddenly he was standing and looking at his love.

"I want you but not like this."

She stared at him as if he had slapped her across the face.

"We will make love but not like this. Please understand."

"I do not. What are you afraid of?"

"Nothing. But I will not leave you like this."

He knelt on the bed over her shimmering body. He breathed in the smell of gardenia, of her. He placed his hand again in the moisture between her legs. He explored with his fingers, feeling her and found the blessed nob and he tenderly rubbed her. Finally, he placed his fingers inside her and she shrieked her release. He kissed her mouth, as she slowly descended from the heights he had taken her.

"I will see you tomorrow. Sleep and wait for me."

"Do not leave me," she whispered. "Please..."

"I must but I will return, later my dear, dear Hannah."

And he was gone.

Timothy's Letter

T*hursday Evening*

Eight o'clock came and went but Timothy did not appear. At a quarter past eight Charlotte came in with a note in her hand.

"It is from his lordship." She handed her the sealed note.

Opening it up, she looked at Charlotte. Her expression showed sadness.

"What does it say Hannah?"

She read it alone.

"My dearest Hannah,

I have unfortunately been called back to my estate on immediate business. I regret I will be away for a week. I ask that you patiently wait for my return. There is still so much I wish to share with you. Tell Mrs. Sarsgard you are to remain under my protection and finances.

I also ask that when I return, you share more of yourself, and I will share all of myself to you.

Your loving and obedient servant.
Timothy"

Mrs. Sarsgard sat on the three-seater lounge.

"This is interesting, is it not?"

"It is but most annoying. We had a real connection last evening, but I fear he does not wish to go further."

"But he does not say that. He says he will return. The truth between you will only strengthen."

"I do hope so. But..."

"Do not fret, Hannah. We just need to keep your mind occupied while he is away. Come..." She stood and took her hand. "I have an extensive library that you may make use of."

The days went so slowly. On two occasions she went for a long walk in St. James Park and Hyde Park. Even Charlotte joined her on the walk-through Hyde Park. Which created a great deal of interest as they walked down the pathways. Men tipped their hats, and some women turned their collective backs to them. Seems Mrs. Sarsgard was well known to her neighbors. But being with Charlotte did not embarrass her anymore. A friendship had grown with the madam, and she was proud to know her.

She also spent valuable time writing to her cousin and telling him things may change for her shortly. And that she would keep him informed. Either she would get Timothy to help her find a position in the country or she would remain here to begin her life as a madam. She had no desire for anything else. If Timothy were well again, she would be very happy. The way he had touched her and given her pleasure told her he was ready to find himself a wife. And that he had an erection was extremely promising.

Reading was her other occupation. Charlotte did have a wonderful library and so she took advantage of many of the books. She even read up on the war that had damaged her Timothy so much.

MISTRESS?

T*he Following Monday Evening*

There was a tap at her door.

"Come."

Charlotte entered the room.

"I have had a note from his lordship. He will be here at eight and asks if you will have supper with him."

"Of course. That is wonderful news. It is not yet a week since he left. It would seem he was able to deal with the issues of his estate more quickly than he thought."

"Yes. Now do you plan to reveal yourself?"

"I did the last evening we had together. Tonight, we continue as friends, or he will depart and never want to see me again."

"You could become lovers?"

"I am not sure if that will be an option, madam."

"Do not rule it out, my dear. I will leave you and arrange for your supper. It is only an hour till he will be here. Would you like a bath?"

"Yes, that is a wonderful idea."

"I will arrange it for you also, my dear."

He came up the stairs. He knew he was grinning like a cat who got the cream. But he was just so excited. Would Hannah be excited? He wanted to marry her as he had wanted over ten years ago.

Would she reveal more of herself to him willingly? Would she marry him despite his issues and scars?

He came to her door and gently knocked.

"Come in," came her sweet voice.

"My dear Hannah. I hope you have forgiven me for standing you up last week." He came to her as she stood before the big chair. He handed her a bouquet of roses, direct from the hot house at his estate.

"Oh Timothy, they are beautiful. But they were not necessary. I know you are a busy man."

"Do you my dear, do you really?"

"Yes Timothy, I do."

He took the flowers from her and laid them on the table. Then he took her in his arms.

"Hannah. The Hannah I fell in love with over ten years ago."

He looked down at her face. His breath caught as he gazed at her beauty. He drew her more tightly into his arms and kissed her. She allowed him to kiss her, so he deepened it. Time stood still as he tasted her. Sweet as honey and just a touch of whisky. My God, he was so in love with her.

She pulled away. "Timothy, you are excited. I can feel your erection against me. This is wonderful news. It means you can find yourself a wife and keep the promise to your father."

"True, but I do not need to find a wife because I have found her."

She heard his words, and her world came crashing in around her. She pulled from his embrace and sat down in the big chair. And she began to cry. She made no sound. Tears flowed down her face. She took in a breath and finally the howl of pain came from her mouth.

"What is this?" He knelt in front of her. He lifted his hand and wiped away a tear.

"I expect they are tears of joy. Who is she?"

"Who is who?"

"Your future wife? I assume that is why you needed to go home so you could organize things and perhaps see her and propose?"

"Well in part, there were things I wanted to prepare. But I am yet to propose."

His smile captivated her. The lucky woman would see his smiling face. She smiled back at him, but the tears still crept down her face.

She suddenly stood and went to the bed and picked up her dressing gown and covered herself.

"I wish you all the happiness in the world, your lordship."

"What is this? I am Timothy, remember?"

"Yes, sir, I am aware of it. But as you are soon to be wed then I would say my job is done."

"But I have not told you who she is?"

She spun around to face him. "I do not want to know who she is. She will haunt me the rest of my life. Now sir, can you leave? Leave!"

She had not wanted to raise her voice. But she had had enough. She would pack her bags and leave and flee to her cousin until she knew what to do.

"But my love..."

"That is the point, I am not your love, am I?"

"Yes, you are."

"Oh, you plan to keep me as your mistress, do you? Well, I tell you I will not do it."

"But I want you and only you."

"Leave," she yelled.

He went to the door and his face looked like she had slapped it a hundred times. It was red and so bitterly disappointed.

He opened the door.

"I will come back when you have calmed yourself, and perhaps then you will listen to me."

He closed the door behind him, and she cried out in pain, and wept thousands of tears.

What had happened?

"She thinks I want another and not her?"

"Your lordship?"

"Mrs. Sarsgard, I am confused. She will not listen to me. I want to marry her, but she seems to think I want someone else."

"Ahh. I understand. She sees herself as no one, sir. She is but a madam now. Not the future wife of a lord."

"I am confused. Why can she not see I have come for her? I told her I loved her."

"Let me guess. She thought you wanted to continue with her being your mistress?"

"Yes, but I said no such thing."

"It does not matter. She thinks she is not good enough for you. She cannot believe you would come to make her a wife."

"But that is ridiculous. It is her I want. I had come to propose to her."

"I do understand but she thinks she is no longer part of your society because she came here to be a madam."

"But I am her only client? Is that not, correct?"

"Yes, but she still sees herself as having descended to a place a real woman would not go. Your lordship, let us have a cup of tea or perhaps something a little stronger while we give her time to come to her senses."

He followed Mrs. Sarsgard down the stairs but it disturbed him to hear Hannah's cries of pain. He had to make this right.

In Mrs. Sarsgard's Office

He could not explain what had happened, so he told Mrs. Sarsgard what had been said.

"It is clear to me what you were saying but marriage was not mentioned. She has assumed the worst."

"Then I will go to her and tell her I wish to marry her."

"I agree."

He downed the last of the whisky and stood, ready to march up the stairs and claim her as his own.

There was a knock at the door. A servant entered and handed Mrs. Sarsgard a note.

"Sit down, your lordship. This is a note from Hannah."

He suddenly was sick to his stomach, as if his life was about to end.

She opened the note.

"Charlotte,

He is well and loves another. I have helped him to heal and of that I am grateful. But you were right. I am in love with him. I cannot continue to work for you knowing how I feel.

Nor can I stay to be his mistress. It would seem, that despite his terrible experiences he cannot change. He was a rake ten years ago and a rake he will remain.

I will have my things sent for, once I know where I will be. I had hoped Timothy would have helped me find lodgings in the country where I could have taken a position as a teacher or seamstress.

I will go to my Cousin Alfred's here in London. Please do not let Timothy know where I am.

Your friend always

Hannah"

"So, this is what she thinks of me? That I would keep her as mistress rather than marry her."

"Your lordship, please see it from her position. She has been in a loveless marriage. A man who used to beat her, rape her and used other women as well. She has always loved you but thinks she cannot have you. Or that you would treat her as her husband did. Her scars and wounds are just as deep as yours. She wanted you to heal but would not allow herself that luxury. Do you understand?"

He leant back into the chair. He did understand and all too well.

"I do, Mrs. Sarsgard. I needed her to heal me and though I have issues we can deal with them, I love her. But I did not consider the wounds surrounding her. What am I to do? If she has left, I cannot tell her I love her."

"I have not told you directly, but you heard where she will be, from her note."

"Alfred's. I know where he lives. In fact, I have been to him to tell him of my love for her. It is right that she goes there. I will see her in the morning."

"Best of luck, your lordship. I await to hear how things will be."

As he left the club, he mentally made a list of the things he would need to convince her of his love for her. He would send a note to Alfred.

It was well after nine when she arrived at Alfred's. She had just a few things with her. Alfred welcomed her with open arms. Even his wife, Nannette, did all she could to welcome her. This both surprised and disturbed her. Once Nannette knew where she had been staying, Hannah had no doubt she would be out on her ear.

"My dear cousin, you can stay as long as is needed. Please make yourself comfortable. The servants will be up here shortly with water for you to wash and tea for you to drink. Come down for breakfast as soon as you are ready in the morning. Sleep well and we will see what can be done tomorrow."

"Thank you, dear Alfred, and thank Nannette again for me, please?"

"I will, my dear. Sleep well."

He quietly left the room, and she sat on the end of the bed. Was her world over? Could she move on, knowing she had been thwarted in love yet again.

A knock at the door brought her hot water she could use to wash, followed by a tray with tea and a shot of whisky. She smiled knowing her cousin had added the whisky. She had developed a taste of it after she had seen Timothy drink it, all those years ago.

She was tired. She washed and then slipped into her nightgown. She sipped on the tea and the whisky. She did not want to think any more. She was heartbroken and convinced she had lost all she had hoped to gain. She slipped into bed and knew that sleep would not evade her.

Breakfast with Nannette

As she entered the breakfast room, Nannette stood and greeted her.

"Come dear cousin and sit here next to me."

Nannette was glowing. Always one for the fashion of the year, her dress was of fine cotton and a beautiful aquamarine. The morning light was dull, and she could see the sky was raining gently out the window behind her. But Nannette was all aglow.

"Thank you, Nannette."

She came and sat next to her cousin's wife. She was slightly fearful of her greeting as the last time they had met, Nannette had made it very clear she did not want her in her house.

"My dear, tea?"

Nannette clicked her fingers and the servant brought over the pot and filled the cup set before her.

A plate of eggs and bread was also placed before her.

"Just eat what you want, dear. I have some fruit also." Another plate with various slices of fruit on it was placed to the side.

"I do hope you slept well?"

"I did Nannette, thank you. A most comfortable bed."

Nannette grinned.

This was most perplexing. What had brightened her cousin's mood?

Hannah nibbled at the bread and the eggs and thanked the Lord above that Nannette had changed.

Alfred entered the room. "You are looking most refreshed, my dear cousin. Which is good news as I have a visitor this morning."

"How does that affect me, Alfred?" she asked. What was happening? Why all this gentleness and hospitality that surrounded her this morning?

"I have a visitor I hope will give you a position in the country." He winked at his wife, who giggled at the comment.

She had no idea what he was talking about but if he had found her a position that would give her an income and a comfortable life, she would be thankful.

"So, who is this benefactor?"

"All in good time, Hannah. You trust me, do you not?"

"Of course, I do. You were the only one who believed me and tried to protect me after the death of Benjamin."

"My dear Hannah," Nannette intruded. She placed her hand on Hannah's. "I had no idea that terrible man had hurt you. I am sorry I did not think about what he was doing to you."

Hannah looked long in the face of Nannette who was not so happy now. She seemed honest in her assertions and Hannah was inclined to believe her.

"Thank you, Nannette, it means a lot to me to hear you say those words."

Nannette lifted her lips into a gentle smile.

"More tea?" She stood and grabbed the pot and topped up her cup and Hannah's.

The rain had stopped, and it allowed her to have some air in the back green area of the house. The flowers seemed to rejoice that they had the refreshing shower. Away from the household gave her time to think. Time to imagine what her life could be like. Teaching and encouraging children. Not her own children but at least... Fresh air and quiet scenery. Not the hustle and bustle of the city. She wanted a family life she could enjoy even if it was not her own family. Now it was just meeting the person her cousin had found to allow her to start a new life. And what work he had obtained for her. The person concerned will arrive this morning. So, she knew she did not have long to wait.

A servant appeared at the door and was about to come out into the garden.

She came toward her.

"Miss, Mr. Alfred requests you come to the library. I have brought you another pair of slippers so you can change those ones. I imagine they are damp from the rain."

"That is most thoughtful of you, Bessie."

She came into the corridor and sat in the chair and took off her slippers. Bessie had provided her with a towel she could use to wipe and dry her feet. And there were her golden slippers. The ones she would wear when she met Timothy in her room. She held them in her hand for a moment. Bessie took the towel and the wet slippers and went on her way.

Timothy. Oh, how she missed him. She wanted to be with him but not as a mistress. But that was all she could be to him. He would never marry a woman like her.

She placed the dry slippers on her feet and headed to the library.

She knocked on the door and heard her cousin say 'enter'. She did. And there before her stood the love of her life, Timothy.

"What is this, Alfred? What is it you plan for me to become?"

"Hannah, please sit down," Timothy spoke clearly and softly.

"Why?"

"Because my dear one, I would like you to hear what I have to say."

She took a deep breath, "For a moment perhaps." She came and sat in the chair near the desk.

Finally, she was calm enough to listen to what he had to say. He smiled at Alfred who turned and left the room. His note to him last evening had made it very clear he was to propose to Hannah this morning but required time alone with her to make his proposal and clarify things between them.

"Hannah, my love..."

"But I am not your love."

"Oh, you most definitely are. You left last night before I could make things clear to you."

"I will not be your mistress."

"No, you will not. You will be my wife."

She lifted her head and looked into his eyes. "Your wife? Who would want me for wife? Do not make me laugh."

He came and knelt in front of her and took her hands into his. He brought her fingers to his lips and kissed them.

"I want to marry you. I have wanted to marry you since the day I met you. But that was not to be. I am sorry for the terrible life you have had with Fredricks. If I could have, I would have freed you from the experience." He lifted her fingers again and kissed them. "But we have both been given a second chance." He wiped away a tear that had fallen from her eye.

"How can we? I am nobody, and you are a lord."

"And I would give it all away if I can spend the rest of my life with you. Please understand. You mean everything to me. You always have but even more now. You gave me your love and healing while I dealt with my demons. You wanted me to heal. That was your goal as it was mine. But I did not think of the pain you were going through."

"How could you? You had no idea who I was."

"That should not have made any difference. You told me you had an unhappy marriage and that you had been beaten. From that moment I should have considered what you had gone through. It was not just me needing healing. You did too."

She cried volumes of tears. Tears that showed she was releasing the pain consuming her. He lifted her into his arms and carried her to the chaise. He kept her on his lap as she cried bitter tears. Just as she had done for him. He held her until she slipped into a quiet sleep, her head resting on his shoulder.

Alfred came in quietly with a tray of tea and nibbles and silently left again not asking any questions or distracting them from what was taking place.

After a time, she woke and looked into his eyes.

"Is it true you want to marry me?"

"It is, my love. I want us to continue healing each other of the things that have given us pain. And for us to concentrate on the love we have for each other and the healing power we will give to each other."

"Marry not mistress?"

"Most definitely."

She buried her head into his shoulder again.

"No more tears, my love. I want us to marry because we love each other."

"Oh Timothy. I love you more than you can know."

"Then that is final. I love you and want you to love me. We shall be happy, my dearest."

"Yes, yes we will."

Wedding

The next weeks were full of events and planning. She had stayed with Nannette and Alfred. They wanted her to leave their home when she married, and she was happy to oblige. After all, she had no home anymore. But soon she would have a large home with her Timothy.

He spared no expense in giving her what she wanted and needed for the wedding. Nannette took great joy in escorting her to dressmakers and milliners and other assorted providers. Her trousseau was building. She was somewhat embarrassed at bringing very little material wealth into their marriage. But Timothy did not care for such things.

Her belongings arrived from Mrs. Sarsgard, with a note.

"My dearest Hannah

I am delighted you and his lordship have found each other again. It was well known many years ago how much he loved you. And many in society were saddened when your parents chose Fredricks to be your husband.

I included. When you wrote to me asking for me to help, I knew

I had to do something. When you came, I only that night decided Timothy was to be for you at last. I could not believe he needed help, and I knew you would be the only one who could help him.

All your belongings are returned. I have included some of the books you were reading and ask that you keep them and remember me as your friend.

I have also included some of the beautiful lace lingerie which looked so beautiful on you. I ask that you and Timothy enjoy them to the full.

Always your friend

Charlotte.

She showed the note to Timothy. And they both agreed she was to be invited to the wedding, regardless of the viewpoints of the *ton.*

Hannah lifted her head from the book as Timothy came through the door of the library. She smiled as he came over and kissed her then sat on the chaise next to her.

"Is it an interesting read?"

"It is and informative."

"Can I drag you away from it?"

"Certainly, my dear. Do we have anything more to organize?"

"No, but I have a special wedding gift I would like to give you."

"Dearest Timothy. You have given me so much already..."

"No not enough, not yet. Now, this will keep you from the house all day. The weather is fine now but a hat and coat may be necessary. I have my carriage which is waiting for us as I speak."

"This is most intriguing."

"All will be revealed."

She departed to her room to fetch her things.

What on earth had he done now?

He had showered her with so many gifts. All she wanted was him. But he took such delight in doing things for her.

Moments later they were in his carriage and off to a secret destination. They left London via the northern road and soon she knew they were heading to her home village of Saffron Waldon in Essex.

"Timothy dear, why are we heading to Saffron Waldon?"

"Because it is there that I have a surprise for you."

"What on earth can it be?"

"Patience, my love. It will be worthwhile."

As they came toward the village, her desire to see her old home was strong. The carriage kept going through the village and did not stop. Then they went right into the driveway that was to bring them to her old home. The one Fredricks had lost due to his gambling.

The carriage pulled up before the house. Timothy helped her down the steps and stood in front of the manor. She looked at him and he handed her the key. The key that would open the front door of her old home. She stared at it in her hand, not sure what she should do.

"It is yours, my love."

"Mine? What do you mean?"

"Exactly what I said. It is yours."

She stared at him speechless. He took her into his arms.

"When Fredricks was trying to sell it, my lawyer acted on my behalf to purchase it. I thought if I could not have you, I could have your home. I had no idea he sold it without you knowing. But I was glad to buy it thinking you would one day perhaps come and seek it out."

"But why my home..."

"As I said it was part of you. Providence knew why. We are to be married at last, so I will give back to you what was taken. My dear, it is yours in name. You may do with it what you will. I have had a caretaker looking after it for years, keeping all spick and span. Now you can decide what you will do with it. But it is yours."

"I am speechless."

She walked to the front door and unlocked it. Stepping inside was like stepping into the past. Memories came flashing into her mind. Her running down the stairs, her mother calling out for her not to run. Everything she remembered about the décor was the same. The furniture looked like the furniture that once stood in the house.

She went upstairs and found her bedroom almost exactly as she left it. She stood there and her mother came to mind again. She had tried so hard to talk her father out of the marriage, to no avail. There were ghosts here but it still was her home.

Timothy came up behind her and placed his arms around her.

"My gift to you. Come here when you need to. If things overwhelm you come here."

"Only if you come too. It needs new memories and dreams. It can be our escape. A place for only us."

"Done."

He watched her carefully. She was quiet but seemed happy.

"Are you happy, my dear Hannah."

"How could I not be? You have given me back my old home. And I love you all the more, for that generous act."

"But...?"

"You know me well. I am waiting to wake up and to see I have been dreaming."

He took her into his arms and snuggled her in close. He placed a kiss on her forehead.

"My darling, this is no dream. We are awake and helping each other mend. Mend from a life that did not agree with us but does so now. Are you happy?"

"More than I can say. I love your generous spirit. We will both heal from our past and grow together in our future.

He gave her a squeeze. She turned to look into his eyes, and he kissed her. This is what he wanted. To love her as she should be loved. Oh, how he waited for the day when they would be together forever.

A Beautiful Wedding

A June wedding had always been one of her dreams. Her wedding to Fredricks had been in December. It was cold and damp and miserable and remained that way throughout the marriage. But today was warm and the sky had fluffy white clouds floating in it. No rain in sight. The carriage gently rocked on the cobbled streets. The sound calmed her.

His carriage had picked her up and she had Nannette as her attendant. Of course, Timothy insisted his carriage with the family coat of arms painted on the side would be used. She would now be Lady Mansfield St James, and he wanted the world to know, he had told her. Nannette had done all she could to make her comfortable in the weeks leading to the wedding. Now, they rode to St Georges Church in Hanover Square. She was about to marry the man she loved.

The carriage pulled up in front of the church. She got out of the carriage and ascended the stairs and waited for Nannette to join her. She looked around at the smiling faces of people who passed by and those who had not gone into the church. People loved weddings and would often stop and see who was to marry. She heard clapping and many of the passersby stopped and joined in the greeting. There was Charlotte smiling at her. She went straight to her and hugged her friend.

"Thank you for coming."

"I would not miss the beginning of this great love story. Enjoy your day and your new life."

"I cannot stop smiling. It is true we are finally coming together. My face aches in such a lovely way."

"And so it will be, for the rest of the day. Now go my dear, Timothy is waiting."

She turned and headed to the door. The doors opened and she stepped inside. At the front of the church the organ began to play, and Timothy stood. He turned to look at her as she made her way down the aisle.

There she is. The most beautiful woman he had ever known. She was an angel. Her dress full of lace and cream material made her glow as she stepped into the church. Her beautiful blonde hair was curled and had white daisies woven through it. But the most special thing of all was she wore a thin cream veil. He knew her meaning and he loved her nod at how they had come together.

Hannah oh Hannah, our dream is finally coming true.

She glided up the aisle to him and he took her hand. He drew her near and lifted her veil.

"I want to see your beautiful face," he whispered as he folded the veil back. Her smile captivated him.

This was the day a new life began. He knew what words he spoke, and he listened to Hannah's reply, but he was not aware that anyone else was there but them. They kept their eyes on each other the entire time.

To the Future

The sun was setting, and a golden glow was spreading across the land. She stood at the window of her new home. A home she would finally share with the man she had always loved. Yesterday had been a beautiful day. The time spent with friends after the ceremony was wonderful. They had rejoiced with her and Timothy for the new life that awaited them. They had food together and danced.

Then she was opening the door to their Mayfair home where at last they made love for the first time. Oh, how exhilarating it all was. His love for her. His desire to please her and have sex a joy and not something to be feared. He caressed her and she him. Oh, how he had taken her to heights and sailed up there with her.

He finally told her why he had pulled away that night at the Soho Club. He had realized he wanted it to be as a married couple. He wanted her to know it was not the club that had given them the second chance but the two of them coming together after lost love. That she had healed him, though he had not expected to be healed.

Hannah smiled to herself. He loved her so much that he wanted to respect their union. And he had. They had driven to the country seat, in Kent, her new home. Drayton House was all she could have imagined. The staff welcomed them and provided a beautiful wedding luncheon to which local families and dignitaries came to celebrate their union. Now as the sun set on their second evening together, she thought of where she would be, the Soho Club. But instead, her Timothy, who had needed saving actually saved her.

Timothy placed his arms around her waist.

"Can I ask you Hannah, what you are thinking about?"

"Dear Timothy. So many things. Our new life together. Our beautiful home and beautiful wedding."

"Is that all?" He chuckled.

She turned to face him. "No, lots of other things. How we again found each other. We will be happy, and we have so much to look forward to."

"We will. I have no doubt there will be times ahead where we remember the things that were not so good in our lives. I will probably still have some bad dreams. But we have each other. The joy is for us now."

He lowered his head and kissed her soft pink lips.

"Those lips are real."

She reached up and kissed him. Time was standing still again. She had no idea how long they stood kissing each other.

Suddenly he lifted her off her feet and carried her to their bed.

"Let us now enjoy each other to the full."

"Fill me, my love, and fill me every day."

"I love you, my Hannah."

She laughed.

"And you, my Timothy."

Love was what they had. She would never forget what they had and how they found each other.

About the Author

Joanne loves to write, and she loves to travel. She is married to Andrew and lives in Central New South Wales Australia with him and their two cats Arthur and Oscar. (Meet them on Joanne's webpage) She has two grown sons and four beautiful granddaughters. Her imagination loves to take her on various trips but mainly in the area of the regency romance.

She also loves meeting new people so do drop a line to her via her Website, Facebook, Instagram, and Twitter.

Acknowledgement

To Ebony for having such a great idea and allowing me to be part of the original Soho Club Anthology, in which this story first appeared.

To the readers who loved this story despite the gloom of its beginning.

To my son Damien for his encouragement in writing this story.

And to my editor, Nas.

And cover designer, Danielle.

From the Author

I have loved using folk law and traditional history in this series. It has spurred my imagination. I love the way the fae have developed in the story and that they too are not perfect and can give a few bad apples to history.

Having mixed marriages was an idea which was there from the beginning but the fae blood would only appear in the females. That too was my idea and I loved playing with it. If you have loved this story, then you will definitely not want to miss the final in the series "Glenna's Future". And please tell your friends about this series.

Keep a look out for it. It will appear later this year.

And just to tempt you here is the cover...

Go to my website and subscribe to my newsletter. It is only monthly so you won't be bombarded by emails.

https://www.joanneaustenbrown.com/

or join me on my Facebook page.

https://www.facebook.com/joanne.boog/

More Books by Joanne Austen Brown

Always Louisa (Always Series Book 1)

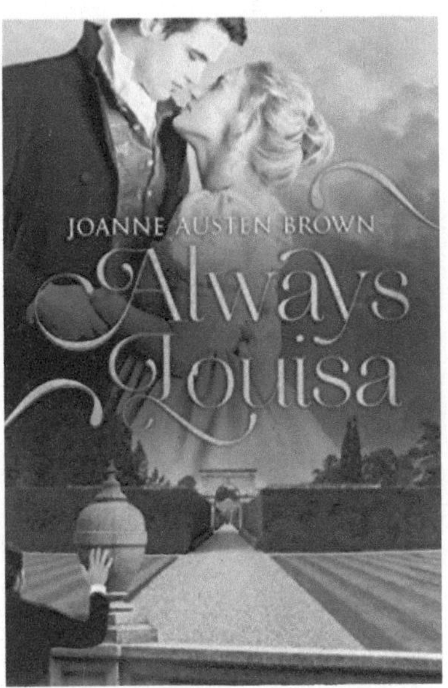

Louisa Stapleton has been disgraced and banished from society. She wants to return to defend herself and seize the life she desires. Her father has obtained the help of the one man she sees as her nemesis. Arriving at the house party, she has her doubts about her success in returning.

Chalanor Farraday, the Viscount Lightford, had a hand in her downfall but he was not a willing participant. To redeem his honour he wants to help her back into the society that rejected her. But she hates him. That is the last thing he wants. Can he convince her to trust him?

Can they overcome the trials that they will face so that Louisa can obtain more than she had hoped for? Neither see the figures lurking in the shadows. They want to prevent her return to society. And they have their reasons for wanting her dead. Will they succeed?

Always Elspeth

Always Elspeth (Always Series Book 2)

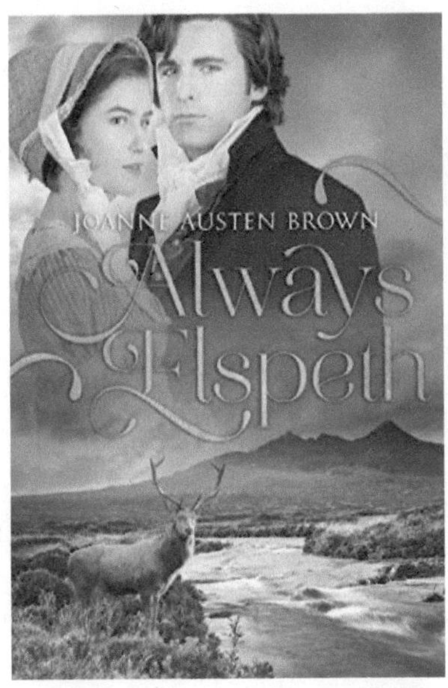

Tragedy has followed Elspeth. Hoping for a new life she moves to the Isle of Skye. Can the society that she hates leave her to start again? What she cannot see is someone who is following her.

James has loved her all his life. Elspeth rejected him once but now she may be tempted to try love again. But in the shadows, someone is stalking her.

Can James and Elspeth renew the love they once had? And make it stronger? Or will the darkness overtake them?

Always Delia

Always Delia (Always Series Book 3)

Delia has been in search for a man she believes is her real father. However, she has been unable to find him. Was her mother telling the truth? Delia decides to go home to the man who raised her and a brother who has protected her.

Lucas has loved Delia almost from the first moment they met. He has done all that he could to help her find her real father. But now he has, he wants to protect her from a man who he knows she will not want to meet.

Their families have been caught up in a twisted tale of love, loss, and villainy. Now they have a chance at real love and a happy ever after. Will it be for Delia and Lucas?

Rachael's Jaunt (Come with Me Book 1)

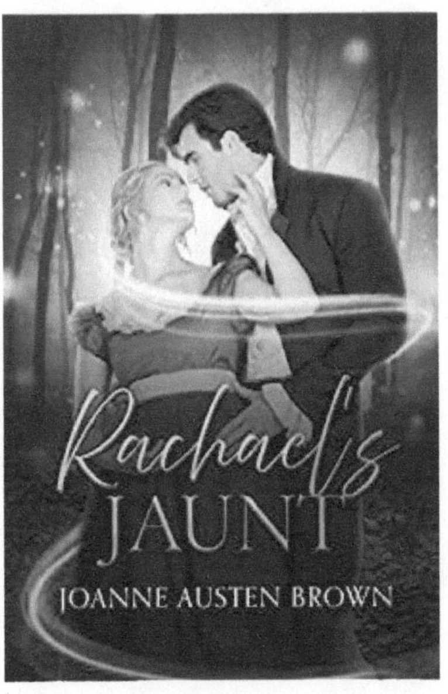

Rachael Fielding loves Scotland. She escapes her busy life for some down time but does not expect that time to be in 1822. Is she dreaming? And why is the man she knows as her dream Scotsman suddenly there in front of her?

Duncan Murray is a laird though he does not want to be. But he was born to the position. Then Rachael shows up and his world is turned upside down. Can she be the love of his life and what have the Fae got to do with it?

Is she a spy for the soon to visit, King George 4th? Can he believe her stories of the future? The two will be tested to their limits. Will the Fae have their way and is there a future for Duncan and Rachael?

Molly's Laird (Come with Me)

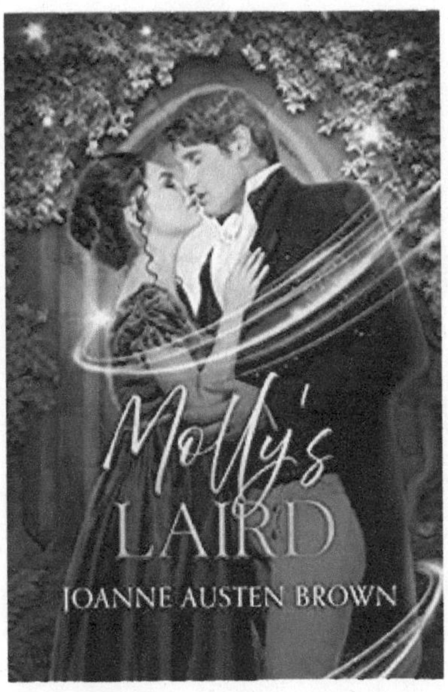

In her own time Molly is a fish out of water. But when she goes back in time to find some peace, after the deaths of all her family, she finds a new beginning.

Can all the promises of the past be true? What about the Fae? And can this handsome man be just for her?

Alasdair misses his brother but understands why he left. He is now Laird but is lonely. Will he find love like Duncan did? Who is the real Molly he cannot stop thinking of? Is she the answer to all he has been searching for? What are the Fae up to?

A Partridge in His Family Tree

A Partridge in His Family Tree

Dianna Partridge rejected him, so he became a rake. But Jason Baird wants to settle down. He needs a woman not a simpering Miss.

Dianna has been running her father business, despite being a woman, and very well. But she feels she has missed out on some things.

Can these two get together and have a memorable Christmas?

The Secret Letter

The Secret Letter

Cora Fitzgibbon appears cold and uninteresting except To Thomas Wright.

He foolishly agrees to be part of a Secret Letter plan invented by his brother. Cold Cora is his match.

But she is not cold or distant and he is very much attracted to her. How can he win her love and keep his promise to his brother.

Love is in the air as Christmas approaches.

Glenna's Future

Coming Soon

www.ingramcontent.com/pod-product-compliance
Ingram Content Group UK Ltd.
Pitfield, Milton Keynes, MK11 3LW, UK
UKHW012252290726
14090UKWH00016B/604

9 780648 775980